WILKINS
the armchair cat

Marjorie Newman
Illustrated by Clare Beaton

Adam & Charles Black · London

Published by A & C Black Limited
35 Bedford Row, London WC1R 4JH
ISBN 0 7136 1860 4
First published 1978
©1978 Marjorie Newman and Clare Beaton
Printed in Great Britain by Sackville Press Billericay Ltd.,
Essex.

Newman, Marjorie

Wilkins the armchair cat.
I. Title II. Beaton, Clare
823'.9'IJ   PZ7.N/

ISBN 0-7136-1860-4

Once there was a ginger cat called Wilkins who had a splendid appetite.

Twice every day, Wilkins would step down from his big armchair, eat a large meal, and drink plenty of milk – to keep up his strength.

Then Wilkins would wash his paws, clean his whiskers, climb back into his armchair, curl himself around, and fall fast asleep . . .

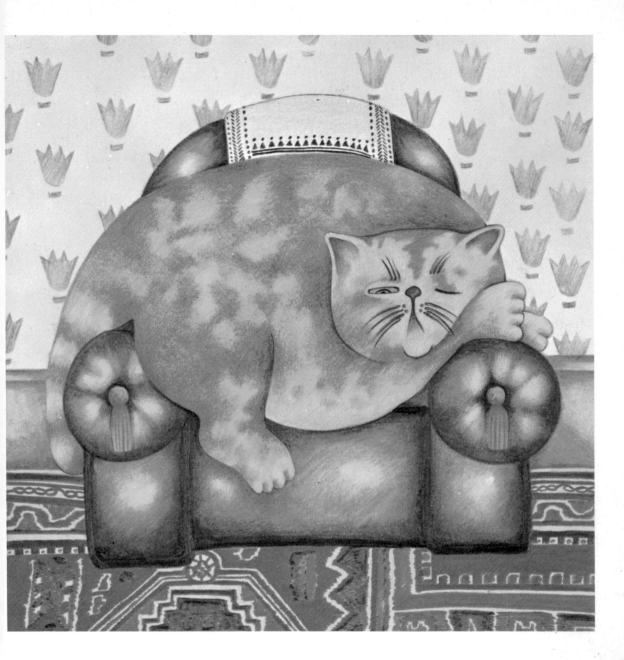

. . . although Wilkins *was* beginning to find it was rather a tight fit to curl himself around in his armchair.

One day, Wilkins felt extra hungry. So he ate an *enormous* meal, and drank *two bowlsful* of milk.

Then Wilkins washed his paws, cleaned his whiskers, climbed up into his armchair, and tried to curl himself around. He tried this way. He tried that way. He tried every way. It was no use.

Wilkins had grown too fat.

'I suppose,' thought Wilkins, sadly, 'I shall have to grow a little thinner.'

Wilkins went into the garden. The window-cleaner was there, fixing up his ladder.

'Perhaps you eat too much, Wilkins,' said the window-cleaner.

'Me! Eat too much!' cried Wilkins. 'Really!'

'Climbing up and down this ladder all day keeps me thin,' said the window-cleaner. 'Why don't you try it?'

'May I?' said Wilkins. 'Thank you!'

The window-cleaner held the ladder steady. Carefully, Wilkins put his paws on the rungs. Slowly, Wilkins climbed. Slowly . . . Slowly . . .

'Hurry up, Wilkins!' shouted the window-cleaner.

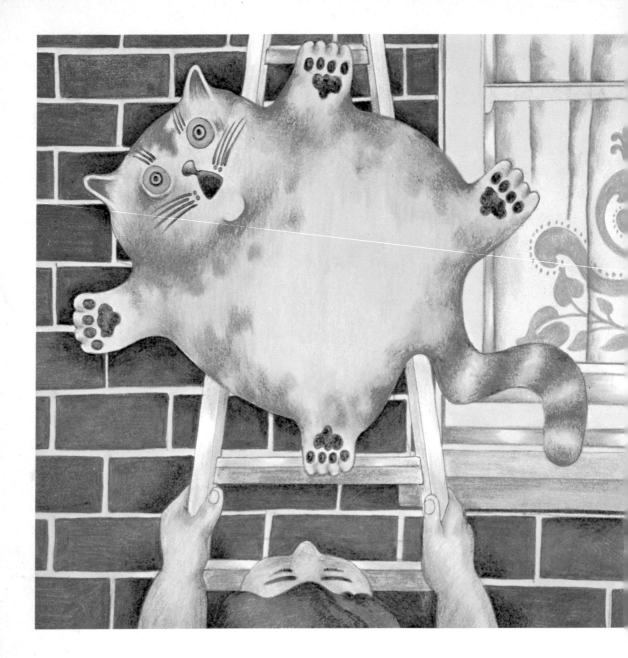

'Meow!' yelled Wilkins, startled. His paws slipped.

Thud! Wilkins landed on the ground.

'Sorry, Wilkins,' said the window-cleaner, running easily up the ladder, 'but I've got work to do.'

Wilkins walked indoors, grumbling.

'No more ladders,' he said. And he was so hungry that he ate a great big meal, and drank plenty of milk – to keep up his strength.

Then Wilkins went to his armchair, to see if he'd grown any thinner. But he hadn't.

'I'll have to try again tomorrow,' he thought, sadly, curling himself around on the rug.

Next day, Wilkins walked along the road. He came to a
jumble sale, and went in. A lady was showing a pair of
corsets to her friend.

    'These would make you look thinner!' she laughed.

    'Excuse me,' said Wilkins. 'May I try them?'

The lady laughed a great deal; but she helped Wilkins to try on the corsets. She pulled the laces tight.

'Meow!' yelled Wilkins. 'I can't *breathe*!'

The lady unlaced him.

'Perhaps you should get more exercise, Wilkins,' she said. 'Or perhaps you eat too much.'

'Me! Eat too much!' cried Wilkins. 'Really!'

Wilkins walked home, grumbling.

'No more corsets,' he said. And he was so hungry that he ate a great big meal, and drank plenty of milk – to keep up his strength.

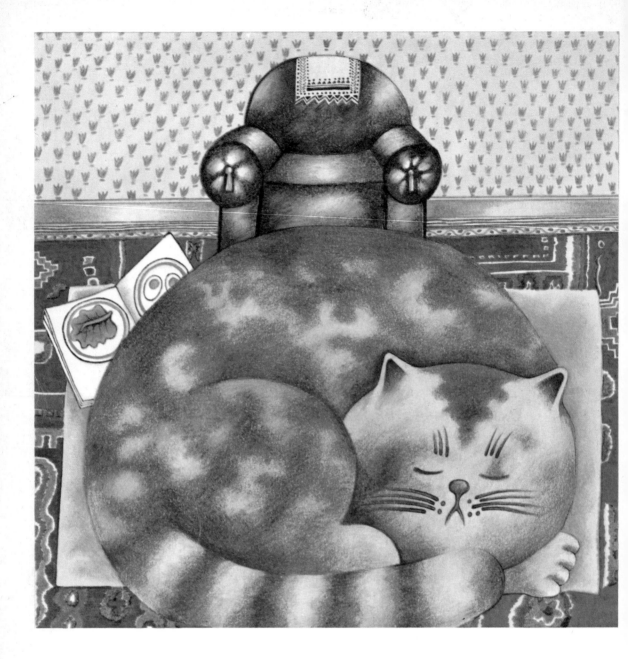

Then Wilkins went to his armchair, to see if he'd grown any thinner. But he hadn't.

'I'll have to try again tomorrow,' thought Wilkins, sadly, curling himself up on the rug.

Next day, Wilkins walked a long way along the road, until he came to a lake. Some rowing boats were moored along one side.

'You're out early, Wilkins!' said the boatman.

'I'm getting some exercise,' Wilkins explained.

'Why don't you try rowing?' said the boatman.

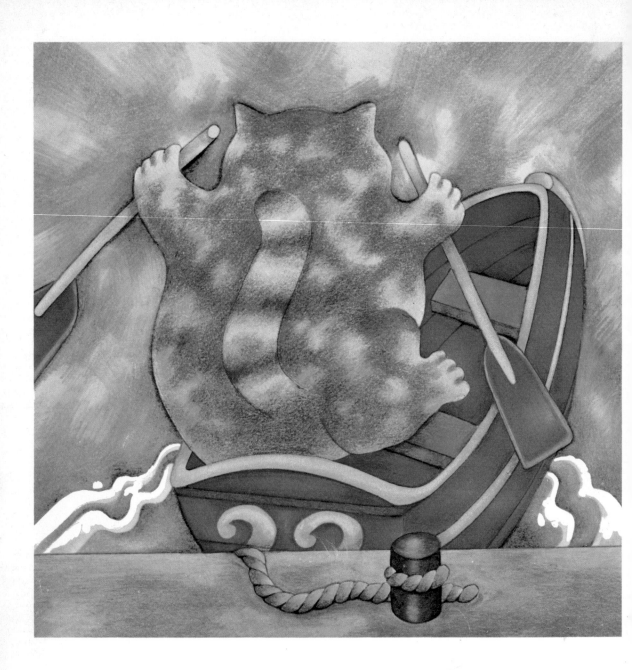

'May I?' said Wilkins. 'But – I haven't any money.'

'Never mind,' said the boatman, kindly. 'No-one else wants to use the boats yet. Just go as far as the island in the middle of the lake, and come back.'

'Oh thank you!' said Wilkins.

Carefully, he climbed into the boat.

Wilkins settled himself, and took the oars in his paws.
The boatman gave the boat a push, and Wilkins started
to row.

'Pff!' said Wilkins, as he pulled on the oars. 'Pff! Pff!
This is very hard work. What a long way off the
boatman looks! Pff! Pff! Meow!'

Wilkins hadn't noticed that his boat was close to the island. Bump! It had knocked against a rock.

'Meow!' yelled Wilkins, startled, losing his oars.

'This boat could be sinking!' yelled Wilkins, leaping across to the island.

'Help!' yelled Wilkins, as the boat floated away.

'I'm stuck!' yelled Wilkins, jumping up and down, waving to the boatman. 'Help!'

The boatman was cleaning one of the boats; and he didn't hear Wilkins.

'Help!' yelled Wilkins, dashing all round the island in case there was anyone else to see him.

'I'm stuck!' yelled Wilkins, scrambling up a tree in case people could see him better from there.

'Meow!' yelled Wilkins, scrambling down again and rushing about in all directions. 'Help! I'm stuck!'

At last, the boatman saw what had happened, and came and rescued Wilkins.

'I'll get the boat later,' said the kind boatman, giving Wilkins a hot drink, to make him feel better.

'No more rowing!' said Wilkins.

When Wilkins reached home, after all that walking, and rowing, and climbing, and running, and jumping, and shouting, and worrying – Wilkins was too tired to think about his meal. He just went straight to his armchair, climbed up, washed his paws, curled around without any trouble at all – and fell fast asleep.